D1477970

. . . for parents and teachers

What is it like to have a mentally retarded sibling?

In *My Sister Is Different*, we see what it is like for Carlo, whose older sister Terry is retarded. At first we learn of the responsibility Carlo must bear — responsibility that leads to resentment toward his sister. It is only after Carlo almost loses Terry that he, along with we the readers, begins to appreciate the special qualities Terry has and the gifts she gives to those around her. In so doing, Carlo discovers the love which underlies his veneer of resentment.

My Sister Is Different, through its simple yet poignant narrative, brings home the point that many of us, like Carlo, are too affected by the things that make retarded people stand out as "different" — and take too little time to discover the talents that retarded individuals may have and the human qualities which *all* people, including the mentally retarded, share.

My Sister Is Different will help children who have mentally retarded siblings, who go to school with retarded persons, or who merely know someone who is "different," to see that while differences do exist, we are more alike, and alike in more important respects, than different. This realization represents a good start toward promoting understanding and respect for those whom society has labeled mentally retarded.

JOHN ANTHONY NIETUPSKI, Ph.D.
ASSISTANT PROFESSOR
DEPARTMENT OF
 SPECIAL EDUCATION
UNIVERSITY OF NORTHERN IOWA
CEDAR FALLS, IOWA

Betty Ren Wright is the author of over forty books
for children. She lives in Wisconsin.

Trade Edition published 1992 © Steck-Vaughn Company

Copyright © 1991 Steck-Vaughn Company

Copyright © 1981, Raintree Publishers Limited
Partnership

Library of Congress Number: 80-25508

   10 11 12   93 92

Library of Congress Cataloging in Publication Data

Wright, Betty Ren.
   My sister is different.

   SUMMARY: Carlo struggles with his positive and
negative feelings about his mentally handicapped sister.
   (1. Mentally handicapped — Fiction. 2. Brothers
and sisters — Fiction.) I. Cogancherry, Helen,
II. Title.
PZ7.W933Mzd   (Fic)   80-25508
ISBN 0-8172-1369-4   hardcover library binding
ISBN 0-8114-7158-6   softcover binding

MY SISTER IS DIFFERENT

by *Betty Ren Wright*

illustrated by Helen Cogancherry

introduction by John Anthony Nietupski, Ph.D.

RAINTREE
STECK-VAUGHN
P U B L I S H E R S
The Steck-Vaughn Company

Austin, Texas

Last year I made a birthday card for my sister Terry. It said:

> Roses are red,
> Violets are blue.
> I like flowers,
> But I don't like you.

I wanted to give it to her, but I decided not to. She's mentally retarded, and she can't read yet. It takes her a long time to learn things.

Terry is older and taller than I am, but I have to play with her every day. Whenever I go outside, Mom says, "Carlo, take Terry with you."

If we play ball, Terry drops the ball. If we play explorer, she crawls around and jumps and swings and runs just like the little kids do. If we play a game, she gets the rules wrong.

The other kids laugh at her. She doesn't care, but I do.

"You should love your sister," said Grandma one day. "Is your heart so dried up and scrawny that it can't love?"

"Maybe it is," I said. I pictured my heart like a crackly brown leaf on the ground.

Grandma shook her head and gave Terry a hug.

9

At Christmas I took Terry to the shopping center to buy Grandma a present.

We saw a powder-puff doll — her skirt had little pockets to hold powder puffs. I didn't know if Grandma would like it, but Terry loved it.

"Pretty, pretty," she kept saying, until the sales clerk stared at us. I bought the powder-puff doll to make her stop staring.

Then Terry had to go to the bathroom. I knew I should take her there, but I was tired of the staring.

"Go up those stairs," I told her. "The door will be right in front of you. I'll wait here."

I watched her go. She stumbled twice on the stairs. She was so excited because she was going all alone.

13

Five minutes went by, and then another five minutes. *She's the slowest person in the world*, I thought.

I decided I'd better go find her. I went up the stairs two steps at a time. I looked all around. She was gone.

"May I help you?" a sales clerk asked.

I told the clerk I was looking for my sister.

The clerk went into the girls' bathroom and came out again. "There's no one in there," she said. "What does your little sister look like?"

"She's not my little sister," I said. "She's older than I am. She's taller than I am."

"I'm sure she's big enough to take care of herself then," said the clerk.

"My sister is different," I said simply.

HOUSEWARES

I walked up and down the aisles, looking, looking.

Terry was lost. What if we never found her? What would my mother and father say?

I knew what Grandma would say. She would look right through me to my dried-leaf heart, and say, "Carlo never did like to play with Terry." And they would all think I had lost her on purpose.

But it wasn't true.

As I walked around the store, I thought about my sister. I remembered the birthday card she gave me last year. It said, "To my dearest brother." Mom had read all the birthday cards to her, and she picked that one just for me.

BROTHER
BROTHER
BROTHER

BROTHER

I thought about how she could make the baby laugh, even when he was teething.

I remembered when she wanted to take my turn doing dishes. Mom wouldn't let her, but she did want to.

I thought about the other kids making fun of her. Then I began to cry. What if someone was being mean to her right then, and she was all alone and afraid?

I started walking faster.

And I almost fell over Terry. She was sitting on the floor with a little boy on her lap. The boy's mother was buying something.

"Is this your sister?" she asked. "She's very good with babies. He was crying his eyes out until she started playing with him."

I wanted to yell at Terry. I almost wanted to hit her. I wanted to tell her how scared I had been.

But I didn't do any of those things. I gave her a hug instead.

"He's a good baby," Terry said. Then she stood up. "Let's go home now." And we did.

I still am not always crazy about looking after Terry every day. I don't always want to take her with me when I go out to play.

But sometimes I think about that day in the store and how I felt when I lost her, and how I felt when I found her again.

This year I made her a birthday card that said, "To a wonderful sister." Mom and Dad said it was beautiful. Terry carried it around for a whole week.

Grandma just smiled. "Well, well. Your heart is in better shape than I thought it was," she said.